Pip and Posy

www.worldofpipandposy.com

First published 2016 by Nosy Crow Ltd
The Crow's Nest, 10a Lant Street
London SE1 1QR
www.nosycrow.com

This edition published 2017

ISBN 978 0 85763 874 8

Nosy Crow and associated logos are trademarks and/or registered
trademarks of Nosy Crow Ltd

A CIP catalogue record for this book is available from the British Library.

Printed in China by Imago.

1 3 5 7 9 8 6 4 2

Pip and Posy

The New Friend

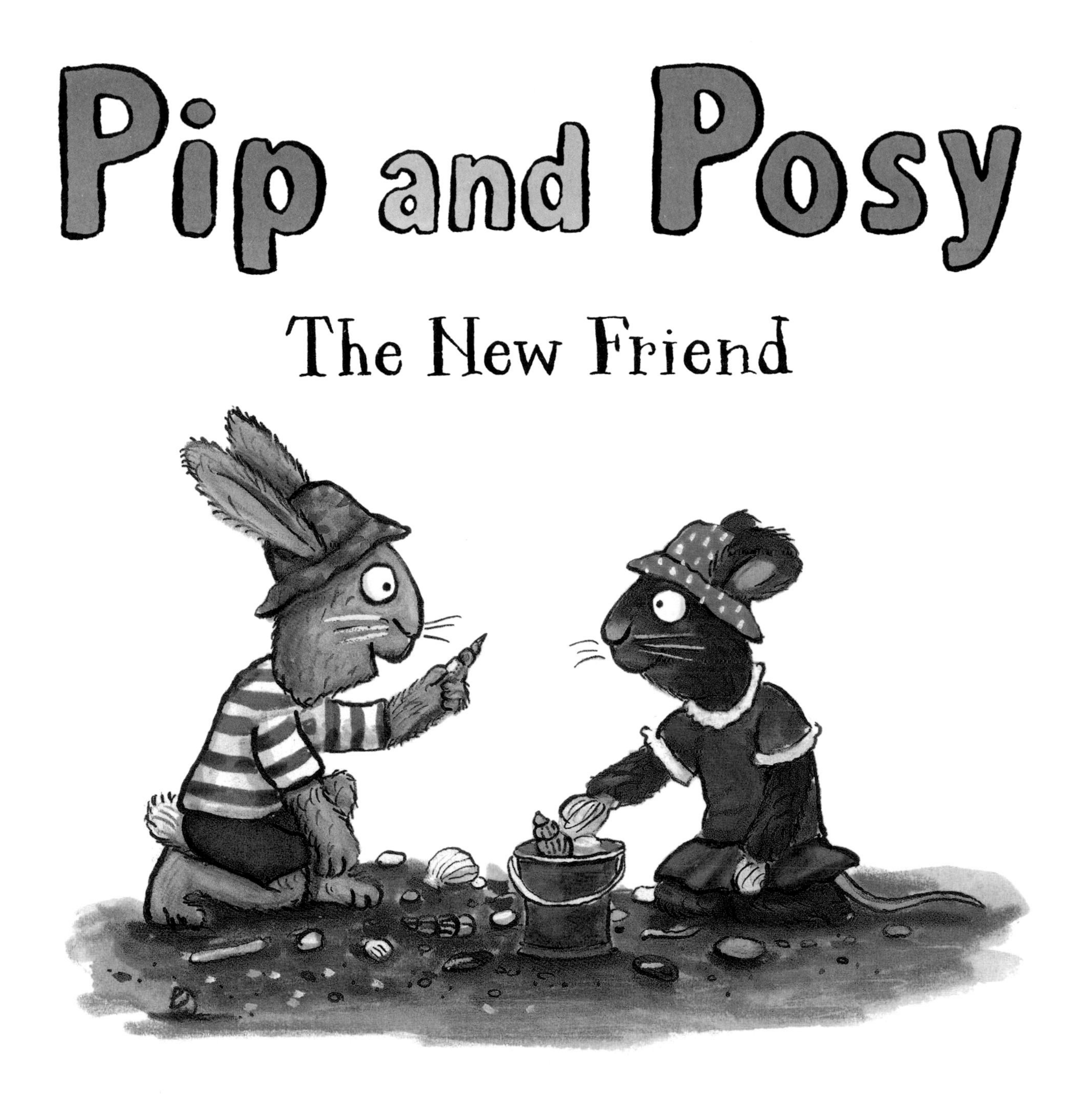

Axel Scheffler

nosy crow

CAR
PARK
BEACH

Pip and Posy were going to the beach.

They unpacked their things.

"Don't forget to wear your sun hat, Pip," said Posy.

They collected shells.

They dug a little hole.

And they paddled in the sea.

After that, Posy had a nap.

Just then, Pip noticed a boy next to them.

“I’m Zac,” said the boy.
“Would you like to play with me?”

“Yes, please,” said Pip.

Zac and Pip played with the beach ball.

They did handstands.

Zac was really good at it!

Zac even let Pip try on
his goggles and flippers.

Pip and Zac were laughing so much
that they woke Posy up.

"Come and play with us, Posy!" said Pip.

But Posy didn't like Zac and Pip's games.

She felt left out.

Then, Zac said that they should go and buy ice creams.

Posy said she would come, too.

But, as they were paying their money, a **bad** thing happened.

A seagull came and stole Zac's ice cream!

Oh dear!

Zac was **very** sad indeed.

Poor Zac!

Then Posy had a good idea.
She gave Zac her last coin so he
could buy himself a new ice cream.

"Thank you, Posy," sniffed Zac.

Pip, Posy and Zac walked back along the beach with the new ice cream.

“What game would you like
to play next, Posy?” said Pip.

Posy thought that they
should all build a
huge sandcastle.

So that's what they did.

Hooray!